SPACE TOURISM

Julie Haydon

Space Tourism

Text: Julie Haydon
Editor: Ben Haskin
Design: Jess Kelly
Series design: James Lowe
Photo researcher: Libby Henry
Production controller: Adam Bextream
Reprint: Siew Han Ong

Acknowledgements
The author and publisher would like to acknowledge permission to reproduce material from the following sources:
AAP Image/AP/Dmitry Lovetsky: p. 18 (Garriott); AAP Image/AP/Mikhail Grachyev: p. 4; AP/Mikhail Metzel: p. 18 (Tito); Corbis Australia: pp. 3, 5, 9, 13, 17, 18 (Olsen), back cover; Getty Images: pp. 1, 6 (inset), 7, 8, 11, 16, 18 (Shuttleworth), 18 (Ansari), 18 (Simonyi), 22 (hotel room), 22 (moon view), cover; PA/EMPICS: p. 21; Photolibrary: pp. 6 (main), 10 (both), 12, 14–15, 19, 23; Picture Media/WENN: p. 20.

Fast Forward Independent Texts
Level 24

For product information and technology assistance,
in Australia call 1300 790 853;
in New Zealand call 0508 635 766

For permission to use material from this text or product,
please email **aust.permissions@cengage.com**

ISBN 978 0 17 017972 0
ISBN 978 0 17 017899 0 (set)

Cengage Learning Australia
Level 7, 80 Dorcas Street
South Melbourne, Victoria Australia 3205

Cengage Learning New Zealand
Unit 4B Rosedale Office Park
331 Rosedale Road, Albany, North Shore NZ 0632

For learning solutions, visit **cengage.com.au**

Printed in Australia by Ligare Pty Ltd
5 6 7 23 22 21

SPACE TOURISM

Julie Haydon

Contents

CHAPTER 1

Space Tourism

Space tourism is the business of taking tourists into space. Space tourists pay huge amounts of money to travel on board **spacecraft**.

In space, tourists can

- look at Earth
- look at the Moon
- feel what it is like to weigh nothing
- visit the International Space Station (ISS)
- carry out research.

a space tourist on board the ISS

Spacecraft are complex machines, and it requires a lot of knowledge, preparation and skill to send spacecraft into space. Opportunities for space tourism are still rare and so far there have been very few space tourists.

The first space tourists travelled to the ISS on board a Russian Soyuz spacecraft.

CHAPTER 2

Human Interest in Space

People have been interested in space for a very long time. At first, people could only observe space from Earth, but recently scientists have learned how to travel into space.

Galileo, an early astronomer, made some amazing discoveries about space.

In 1969, astronauts landed on the Moon for the first time. People around the world watched the Moon-landing on television. They saw astronaut Neil Armstrong step onto the Moon and heard him say, "That's one small step for man, one giant leap for mankind." The Moon-landing made a lot of people interested in going to space.

the first Moon-landing in 1969

CHAPTER 3

Preparing for a Trip into Space

Travelling into space is not like normal travel. Before people can be space tourists they must be checked by doctors to make sure they are healthy and fit enough for space travel.

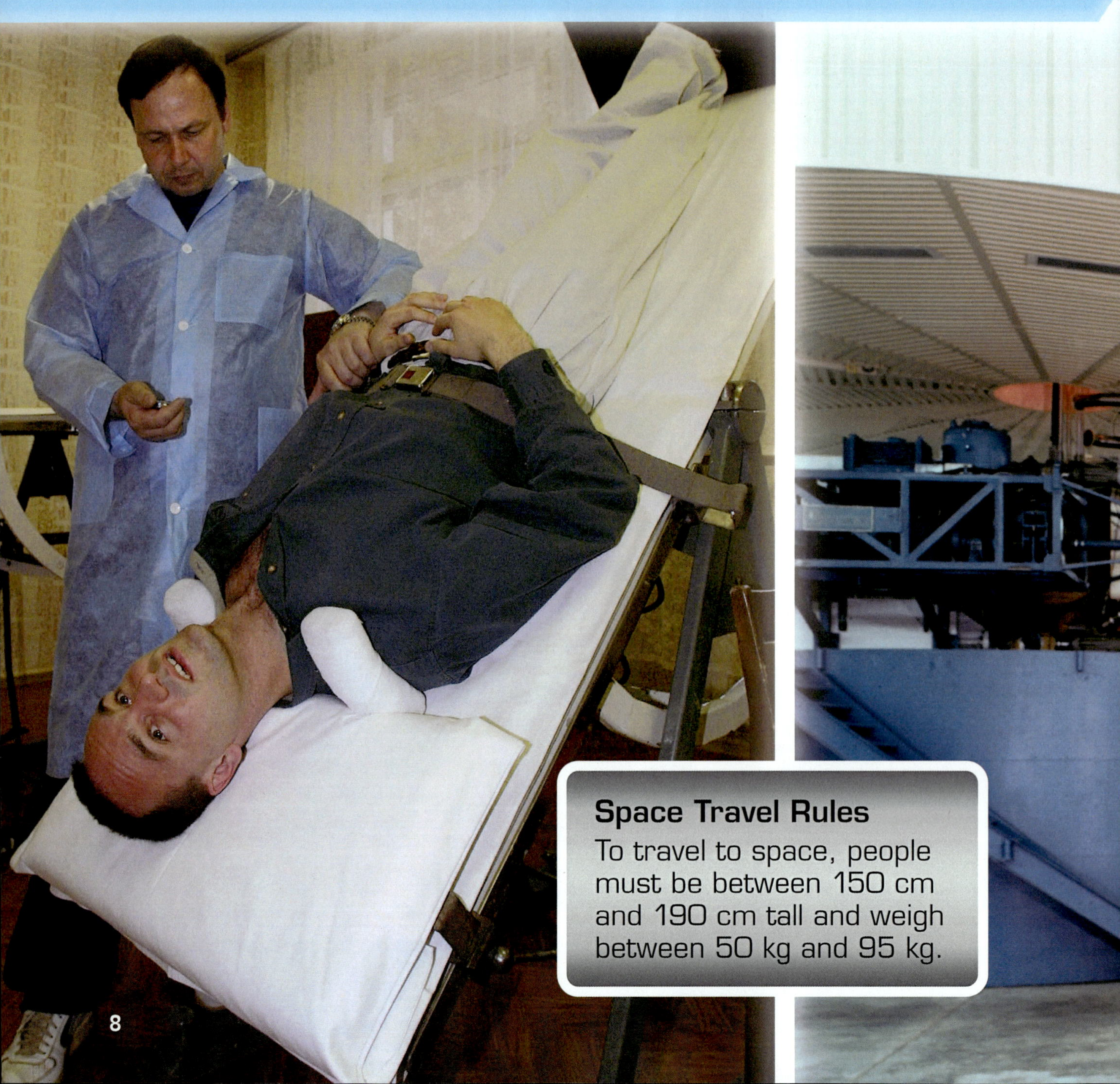

Space Travel Rules

To travel to space, people must be between 150 cm and 190 cm tall and weigh between 50 kg and 95 kg.

Space tourists also need to prepare for the journey. They need to learn a lot of new skills and get used to the conditions that they will face on the trip.

Space travellers train inside special machines to get used to the extreme acceleration their bodies will experience during lift off.

CHAPTER 4

Being in Space

Being in space is very different from being on Earth. Everything that people need, such as air, water and food, must be brought into space from Earth, or made in space. People must also be protected from the conditions in space, such as extreme heat and cold.

*A lot of the food that space travellers eat on their trip is **dehydrated**. They must add water to the food before they can eat it.*

Microgravity

A space station is kept in **orbit** by Earth's gravity, but the effects of gravity are not the same in orbit as they are on Earth. This is because the space station is **free-falling** continuously around Earth. The space station and the people and objects inside it are all falling at the same speed, so the people and objects float. This state is called microgravity.

a space tourist in free-fall

Free-Falling

Many people want to travel in space to feel what it is like to free-fall. People in free-fall weigh nothing. People on Earth can free-fall for a short time on some roller-coaster rides.

Some people feel sick for the first few days that they are in microgravity. Being in microgravity is also bad for the muscles and bones. Because people in space float around, they do not use their muscles much. People on the International Space Station need to do special exercises to stay in shape.

Space Exercise

People on the ISS use a special exercise bike as part of their exercise program. The bike has a special harness to stop the user from floating away.

Microgravity affects all parts of life on the ISS, from eating to going to the toilet.

Liquid Salt

Salt and pepper are served as liquids on the ISS. This is so that grains of salt and pepper do not float away and damage the equipment on board.

The International Space Station

A space station is a place where people can live and work in space for a long time. There is only one space station at the moment – the International Space Station.

Space tourists usually visit the ISS for about two weeks, but astronauts can live there for many months.

The ISS **orbits** Earth. As it moves around Earth, it shows different views of the planet to those on board.

The ISS is in use now. Most of it was completed by 2011, but there are parts of it that are not built yet.

Each part of the ISS is made on Earth. Then the parts are transported into space by spacecraft and are put together by astronauts, **cosmonauts** and robots.

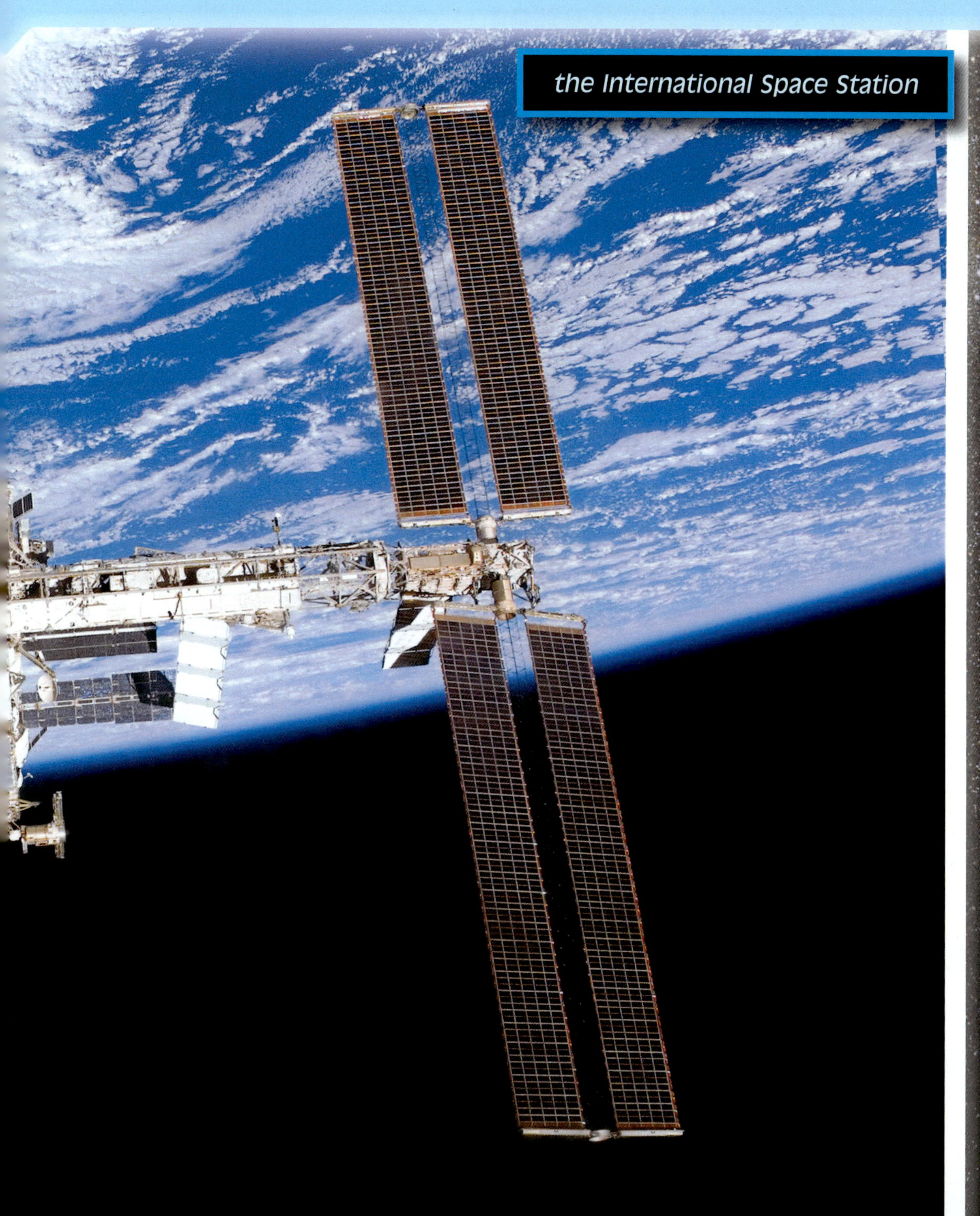

the International Space Station

The main jobs of the astronauts and cosmonauts on the ISS are to continue building the station, to take care of it and to do research.

Spacecraft carry astronauts and space tourists to the ISS and bring them home again. The ISS is run by NASA in the USA, the Federal Space Agency in Russia, and space agencies in Japan, Canada and Europe.

an astronaut doing maintenance work on the ISS

Most space tourists have a lot to do when they are on the ISS. Space tourists usually carry out research while they are there.

An excellent thing to do on the ISS is to look at the view. Earth looks very beautiful from space.

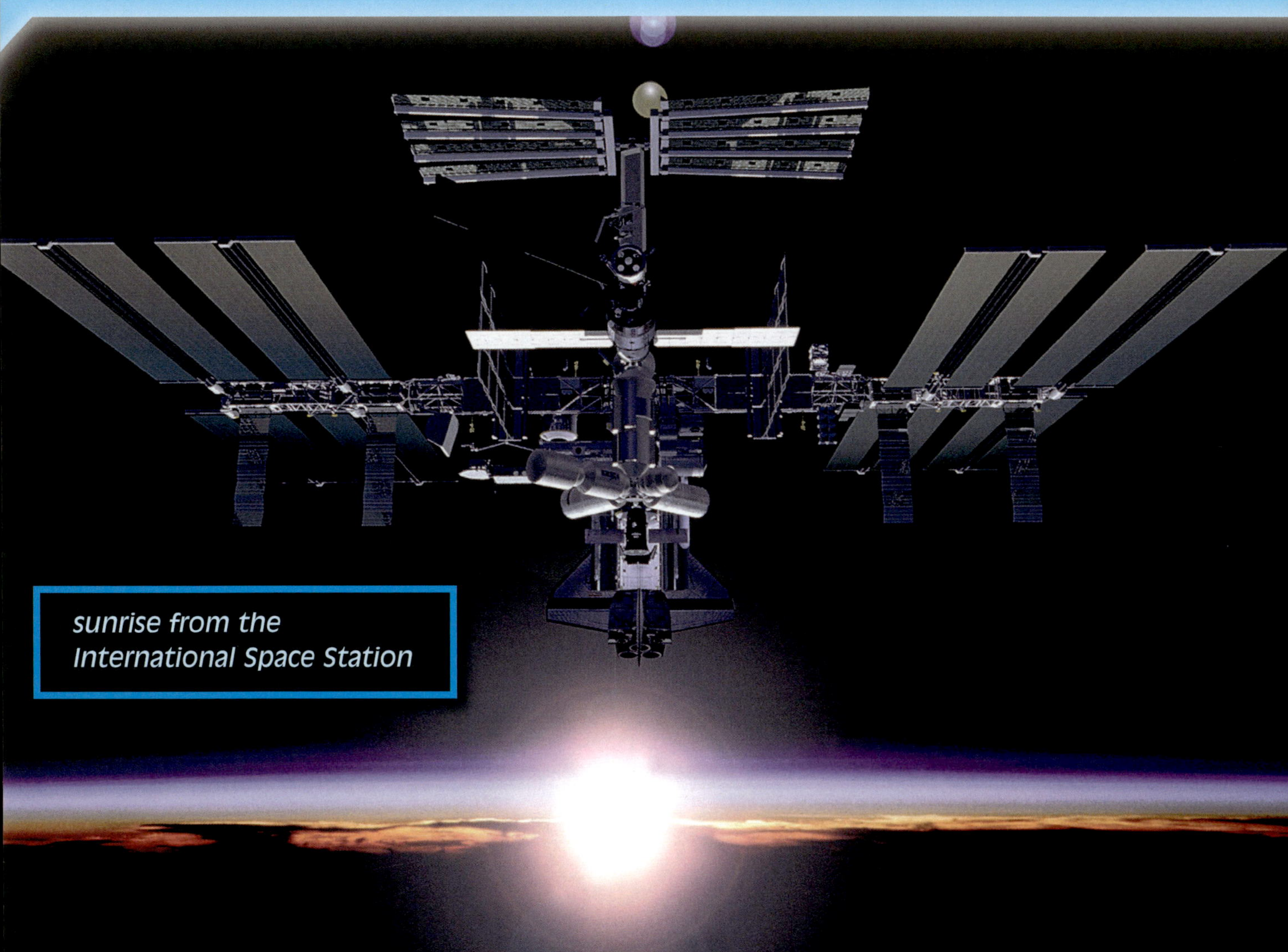

sunrise from the International Space Station

What Day Is It?

Space tourists can see 16 sunrises and sunsets for each day they spend on the ISS. This is because the ISS goes the whole way around Earth once every 90 minutes. So every 45 minutes the people on board can see a sunrise or a sunset.

CHAPTER 5

Space Tourists on the ISS

So far, only a few space tourists have been to the ISS. This is because space tourism is expensive. Also, most seats on spacecraft travelling to and from the ISS are kept for astronauts and cosmonauts to use. As new spacecraft are built, space tourism will increase.

The Space Tourists

1. Dennis Tito

Nationality
American

Journey dates
28 April – 6 May 2001

2. Mark Shuttleworth

Nationality
South African-British

Journey dates
25 April – 5 May 2002

3. Gregory Olsen

Nationality
American

Journey dates
1–11 October 2005

4. Anousheh Ansari

Nationality
Iranian-American

Journey dates
18–29 September 2006

5. Charles Simonyi

Nationality
Hungarian-American

Journey dates
7–21 April 2007
26 March – 8 April 2009

6. Richard Garriott

Nationality
American

Journey dates
12–23 October 2008

The First Space Tourist

American businessman Dennis Tito was the first space tourist. He visited the ISS in 2001. He was very interested in space travel, as he had worked as a space scientist for many years.

Dennis had to do 900 hours of training over many months at a special cosmonaut training school in Russia.

Dennis finally took off on 28 April 2001. He spent six days on the ISS.

Dennis described going into space as a **spiritual** journey. He returned to Earth on 6 May 2001.

CHAPTER 6

Space Tourism in the Future

Some businesses are building spacecraft to take tourists on short trips beyond Earth's atmosphere to where space begins. These spacecraft will not go into orbit.

Some businesses also plan to use their own spacecraft to take tourists on longer trips into space.

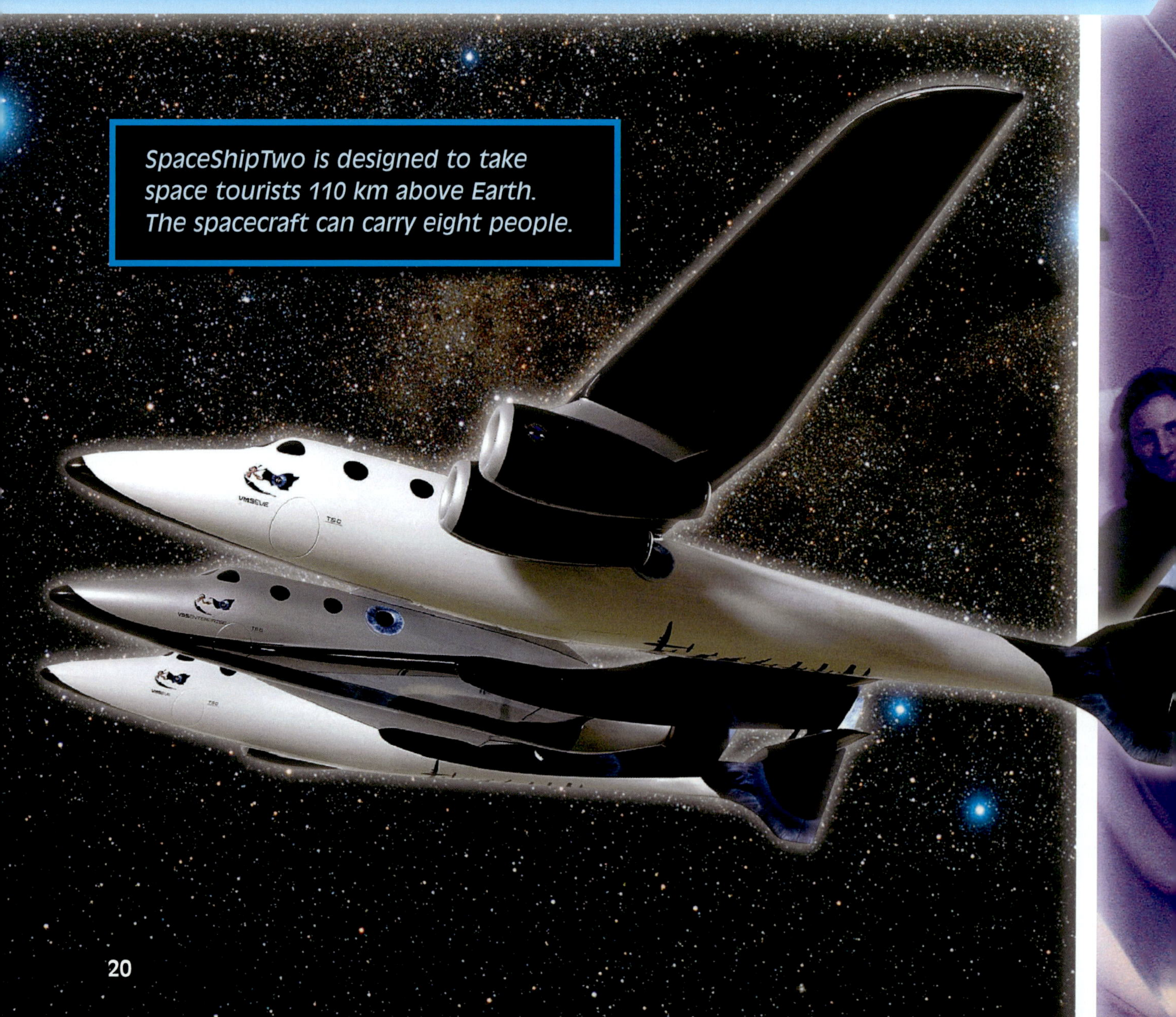

SpaceShipTwo is designed to take space tourists 110 km above Earth. The spacecraft can carry eight people.

Space tourism businesses need to focus on safety, comfort and fun. Their spacecraft must be able to fly tourists into space and return them safely to Earth. The trip must be comfortable and exciting or people will not be interested in buying tickets.

inside SpaceShipTwo

In the future, space tourists may be able to take **spacewalks** outside the ISS or on the Moon. They may be able to stay at space hotels or to holiday on the Moon. Far in the future, space tourists may even be able to visit other planets.

An artist's idea of what a holiday on the Moon might be like.

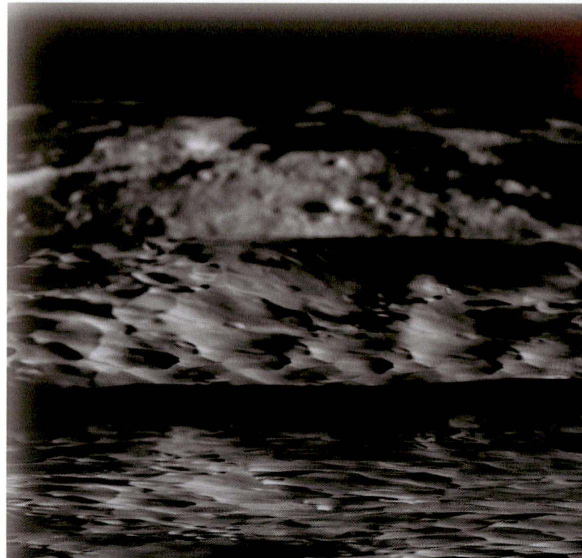

The things that people learn from space tourism may help them to think of ways to **colonise** the Moon or the planets, and to find ways for people to live in space for longer periods.

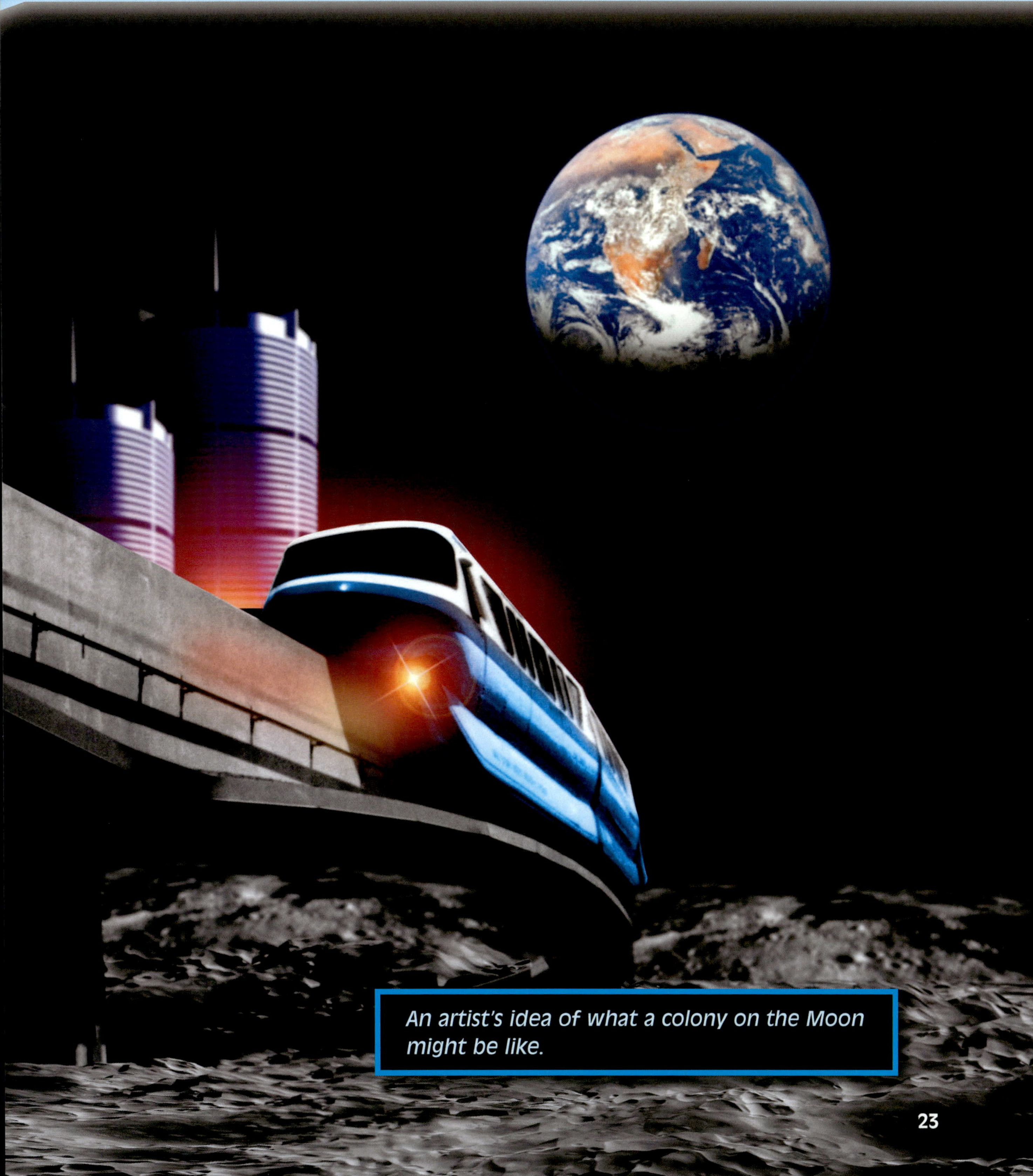

An artist's idea of what a colony on the Moon might be like.

Glossary

colonise to set up a long-term settlement in a new place

cosmonauts the Russian term for astronauts

dehydrated dried out

free-falling moving only due to the force of gravity

orbit the path that an object in space follows around a larger object

orbits moves around a large body in space, such as a planet

spacecraft vehicles used for travel in space

spacewalks activities performed in space outside a spacecraft

spiritual to do with the spirit or soul

Index